Designed by Flowerpot Press in Franklin, TN.
www.FlowerpotPress.com
Designer: Stephanie Meyers
Editor: Katrine Crow
ROR-0808-0103
ISBN: 978-1-4867-1257-1
Made in China/Fabriqué en Chine

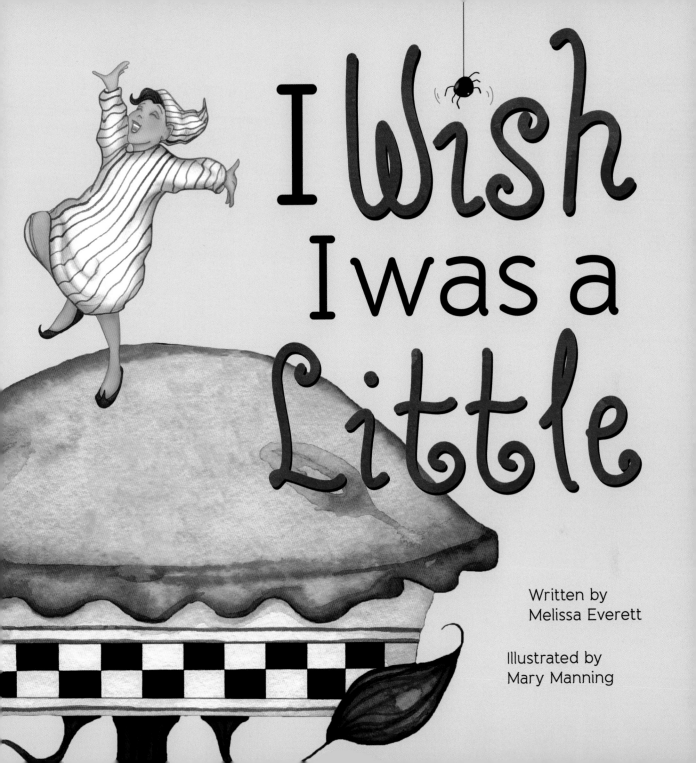

I Wish
I was a
Little

Written by
Melissa Everett

Illustrated by
Mary Manning

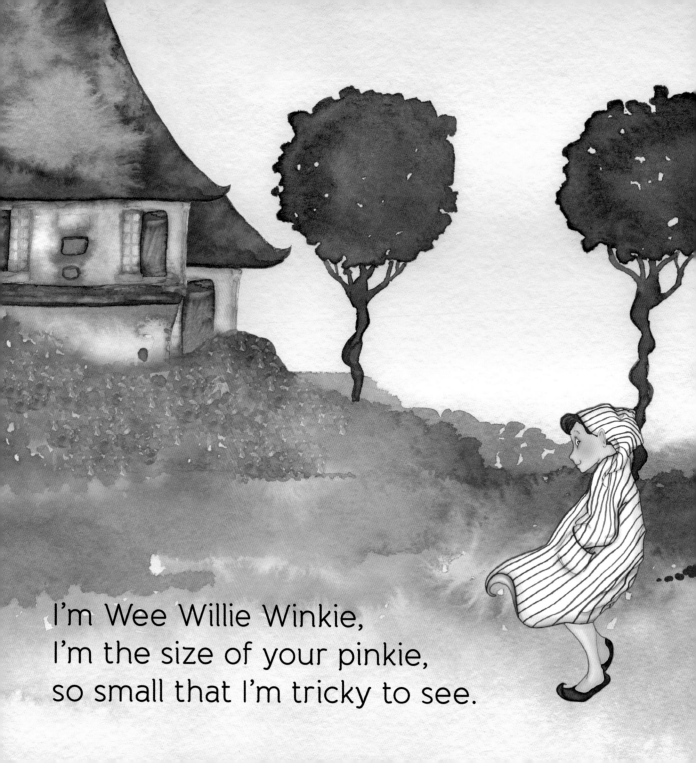

I'm Wee Willie Winkie,
I'm the size of your pinkie,
so small that I'm tricky to see.

I want to be loved,
like all of the littles
so that everyone sings about me!

I wish I was a little
like Little Jack Horner
and you sing about just where I sit.

I wish I was a little
like This Little Piggy
and you wiggle me and say I am it.

I wish I was a little
like Little Boy Blue
so I could go blow my horn.

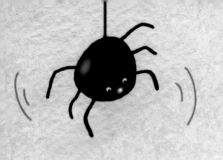

I wish I was a little
like Little Miss Muffet;
I would lay down and sleep until morn.

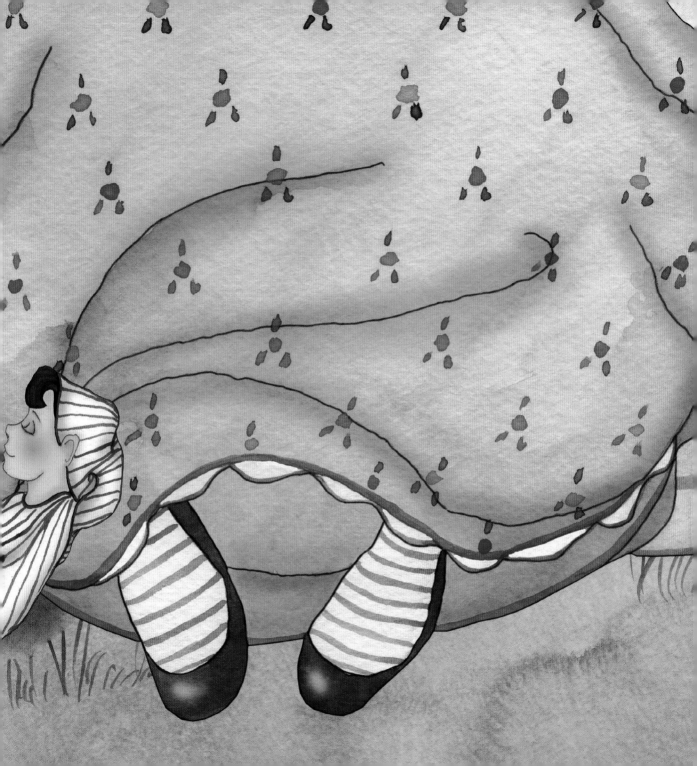

I wish I was a little
like Mary's little lamb
with fleece as white as snow.

Then you could sing songs
about where I am
and where I am sure to go.

But I'm not a little.
I'm Wee Willie Winkie.
I'm smaller and harder to see.

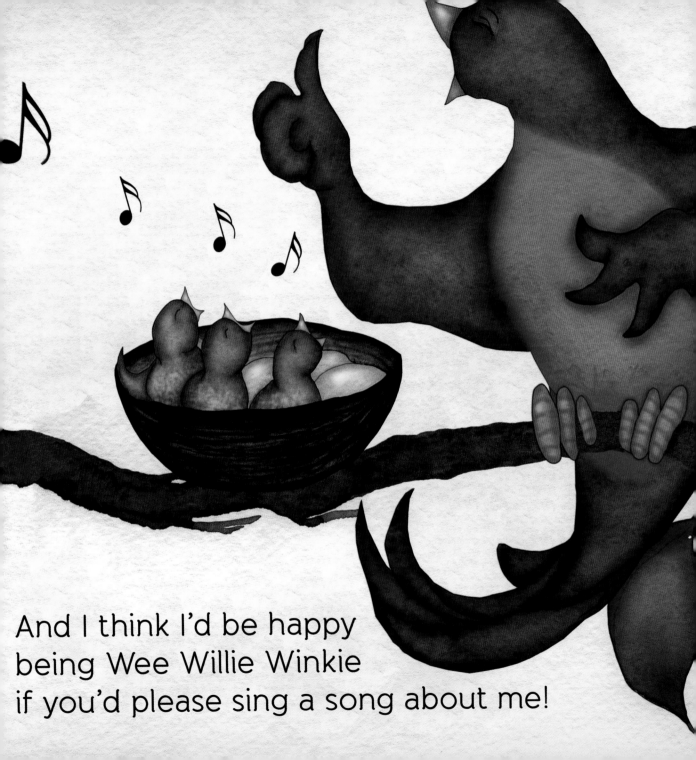

And I think I'd be happy
being Wee Willie Winkie
if you'd please sing a song about me!